BOSTON PUBLIC LIBRARY

ROZ
and
OZZIE

By Johanna Hurwitz

The Adventures of Ali Baba Bernstein
Aldo Applesauce
Aldo Ice Cream
Aldo Peanut Butter
Baseball Fever
Busybody Nora
Class Clown
Class President
The Cold and Hot Winter
DeDe Takes Charge!
"E" Is for Elisa
The Hot and Cold Summer
Hurray for Ali Baba Bernstein
Hurricane Elaine
The Law of Gravity
Much Ado About Aldo
New Neighbors for Nora
Nora and Mrs. Mind-Your-Own-Business
Once I Was a Plum Tree
The Rabbi's Girls
Rip-Roaring Russell
Russell and Elisa
Russell Rides Again
Russell Sprouts
School's Out
Superduper Teddy
Teacher's Pet
Tough-Luck Karen
Yellow Blue Jay

ROZ
and
OZZIE

Johanna Hurwitz

ILLUSTRATED BY
EILEEN McKEATING

MORROW JUNIOR BOOKS
NEW YORK

acc
8-28-92
FIELDS CORNER

Printed in the United States of America.
1   2   3   4   5   6   7   8   9   10

Library of Congress Cataloging-in-Publication Data

Hurwitz, Johanna.
    Roz and Ozzie / Johanna Hurwitz ; illustrated by Eileen McKeating.
        p.   cm.
    Summary: Although eight-year-old Roz usually feels annoyed by the pestering attentions of her uncle Ozzie, who is two years younger than she is, she finds that there are times when she is glad to have him around.
    ISBN 0-688-10945-4 (trade)
    [1. Uncles—Fiction.   2. Family life—Fiction.]   I. McKeating, Eileen, ill.   II. Title.
PZ7.H9574Ro   1992
[Fic]—dc20   91-42338   CIP   AC

*Especially for
Robina Gordon Frank:
"Bobbi"*

Contents

ROZ
and
OZZIE

1

A Fuss on the Bus

It was twenty minutes past three on a Tuesday afternoon, and Rosalind Sasser was sitting on the front seat of the school bus. Next to her sat Brie Morgan, who was in Roz's fourth-grade class. Brie lived on a different bus route, and this was the first time she had gotten permission to take the bus home with Roz.

"I'm so glad you're coming to my house today," said Roz as the bus moved down Kinkade Avenue toward her home.

"Next time it will be your turn to come with me," said Brie.

Roz beamed with pleasure. She liked Brie

and hoped they would become good friends. It was only the third week of school, and Roz was new in town and new at Sullivan School. She had already signed up for Girl Scouts, but she was looking for a special friend. So far, the only person she really knew was a second-grade boy, Ozzie Sims. Most days Ozzie squeezed into the bus seat next to Roz whether she liked it or not. They lived next door to each other, and from the day Roz had moved in, Ozzie had moved into her life, full-time. Thank goodness he was sitting in the back of the bus today with some other kids his own age. He could be an awful nuisance.

"I want my mother to see your earrings," Roz told Brie. "She thinks eight is too young to get your ears pierced, but now I'm almost nine. And yours look so neat. Maybe she'll say yes after she sees yours."

Brie smiled and shook her head so her long brown hair moved to show her ears and the tiny pieces of jewelry she was wearing.

Suddenly the girls heard a big commotion in the back of the bus. There were shouts and cheers from the children sitting behind them. Roz and Brie turned around to see what the fuss was all about. Some children were out of their seats and others were shoving and pushing them. Many of the children were yelling and grabbing things off the floor.

"What happened?" asked Brie.

Roz shook her head. She had no idea.

The bus pulled to the side of the road and stopped. The tall bus driver everyone called Smiling Jack got out of his seat and faced the students. He was not smiling.

"Just what do you think is going on?" he roared. "The first rule of riding on a school bus is that you stay in your seats."

"Yeah. But it's raining money back here!" someone shouted.

"I don't care what it's doing. It can be raining pigs for all I care. This bus isn't moving an inch until you're all back in your seats."

"Look what I found," a boy yelled out. "Fourteen, fifteen, sixteen cents," he counted. "There's a million pennies back here."

"It's not a million. And they're mine," a small voice called out.

Roz cringed as she recognized the voice. It was Ozzie Sims. She should have guessed that if there was trouble, Ozzie would be in the middle of it. She wished there was a way that she and Brie could avoid him when they got off the bus. It would probably be impossible to make friends with anyone with Ozzie under foot.

"I've got a hole in my pocket and my pennies fell out," Ozzie said. "So you better give them back to me."

"Finders keepers, losers weepers," said the boy with the sixteen cents.

"I didn't *lose* my pennies. They just fell on the floor of the bus. But I know where they are and you better give them back to me. Collecting pennies is my hobby," said Ozzie.

"Driving a bus is not my hobby," shouted Smiling Jack. "It's my job. And if you kids want to get home this afternoon, you better settle this business and settle it fast."

"Give him his pennies," a girl called out.

4

"Otherwise, I'm going to be late for my piano lesson."

"I have to go to the dentist," someone else yelled. "I'll be glad if we're late."

"Wow," said Brie. "Do you have things like this happen on your bus every day? My bus is pretty boring. We just drive along until we get home."

Roz shrugged her shoulders. Last week Ozzie had dropped a container of orange juice as he got on the bus. He should have finished it at lunchtime. Smiling Jack didn't allow you to eat or drink on his bus. The spilled juice had made a mess, but at least it hadn't delayed the kids getting home.

"There's not much you can buy with pennies these days," said Smiling Jack now. "So I suggest you all give Ozzie his money back and we get this bus on the road."

One by one the kids handed over the pennies they had picked up off the floor of the bus.

"Do you have them all now?" the driver asked Ozzie.

"I didn't count them yet," said Ozzie. "If

you find any when you take the bus in at the end of the route, will you save them for me?"

"Sure," said Smiling Jack. "Like I said, there's not much you can do with a handful of pennies."

Everyone got back in their seats and the bus pulled away from the curb. It was just another couple of blocks till they reached Roz's corner. She hoped they'd get there without another mishap. Otherwise it would be time for Brie to go home by the time they got to Roz's house.

Finally the bus slowed to a halt at the corner of Kinkade and Corn. "This is it," said Roz.

Only one other person got off at the same stop with them. Ozzie Sims.

Roz would have liked it if she and Brie could have walked along Corn Street alone. There are lots of things girls want to talk about without a boy listening in. But Ozzie walked along right next to them.

"How come *she* got off the bus with you?" Ozzie demanded to know, pointing at Brie.

"She's my friend," said Roz. "And we would like a little privacy, if you don't mind."

But of course Ozzie minded. He did not take the hint and kept pace with the girls. You could hear his pennies jingling together inside his backpack. Roz sighed in resignation.

"This is Oscar Sims, but everyone calls him Ozzie," Roz told Brie. "He always follows me around. Our families live in the same two-family house."

Ozzie's freckled face grinned proudly at this accomplishment of his.

"Do you think you got all your pennies back?" asked Brie.

"I hope so," said Ozzie. "But the good thing is that my valuable pennies are at home. I just like to carry my extra ones around with me. When we get home I could show you my best penny. It's a different color from regular pennies. It's gray, because it's made out of zinc."

"I thought pennies were all made out of copper," said Brie.

"In 1943, during World War II, they

made all the pennies out of zinc, because they didn't have enough copper."

"Is it really valuable?" asked Brie. "I mean, is it worth a lot of money?"

"By the time I'm grown-up, it will be worth loads."

"You're weird," Roz told Ozzie. "I never heard of anyone getting so excited about a penny."

"That's because you don't collect them. I have four hundred and eighty-six pennies now. They all have the year they were made on them. But others also have the letters *D* or *S* on them. It means they were minted in Denver or San Francisco. It's exciting to think that a penny you touch has traveled all over the United States. My pennies have been everywhere in the whole country."

"Do you know what?" Roz said, turning to Brie. "He asked his mother to give him his allowance in pennies. So every Friday she has to go to the bank to get him a roll of pennies."

"It's fifty cents," said Ozzie. "And some weeks I get a new penny that I need for my collection. It's getting harder and harder to find a wheat penny. Those are pennies that have two pieces of wheat on the back. They stopped making them and soon they are going to become valuable, too. The good thing for me is that most people don't know, and so they spend them. When I'm lucky, I find one in my allowance."

"I told you he was weird," said Roz, looking to Brie for support.

"Someday when I'm very rich you won't be laughing," said Ozzie.

"I'll believe it when I see it," Roz scoffed. "And in the meantime, you ought to stop carrying all those pennies around with you. It's no wonder the weight of them made a hole in your pocket."

"I like the feel of them," said Ozzie. He turned to Brie. "Do you want to hear a riddle?" he asked her.

"No," said Roz.

"I didn't ask you," said Ozzie. "I asked her."

Brie shrugged her shoulders. "I don't care," she said.

"Why did the duck cross the road?" he asked.

Brie shrugged her shoulders again.

"It was the chicken's day off," said Ozzie, grinning.

"Ozzie. That's just plain stupid," complained Roz.

"I have another one," said Ozzie, ignoring Roz. "Why did the dinosaur cross the road?"

"It was the chicken's day off," guessed Brie.

"Nope. Chickens weren't invented yet," said Ozzie, laughing. He loved his riddles almost as much as his pennies, and he came up with new ones almost every day.

"That's even more stupid than the other one," said Roz.

"What are we going to do this afternoon?" Ozzie asked.

"Brie and I are going to do our homework together," said Roz. "I don't know what you are going to do."

"Why don't you come and play at my house for a while before you do your homework?" offered Ozzie. "You could pick whatever game you want."

"No. We have to do our homework.

Fourth grade is much harder than second," Roz bragged.

"It really is," Brie said to Ozzie. "You'll find out when you get there."

"We could ask Mrs. Menzer if she'll let us walk her dog," suggested Ozzie. Mrs. Menzer was their neighbor. She often let the children take her poodle, Samantha, for her afternoon exercise.

"I'll let you both hold the leash before I do," Ozzie said.

"I told you—we have a lot of homework," said Roz. She always told Ozzie that when she wanted to avoid him.

"Can I come and watch while you do it?" asked Ozzie.

"Watch us do homework? We're not a TV show," said Roz. "You can't just come and sit and watch us. Besides, you'll make too much noise and we won't be able to think."

"I'll be quiet. I promise," said Ozzie. "And then when you're done we can do something together."

"N-o spells no," said Roz. "Go find someone your own age to play with. You don't have to follow me everywhere."

"But I like to do things with you," said Ozzie. He let out a long sigh. "I guess I'll walk Samantha by myself. But if you change your mind and you want to play with me, I'll be ready."

Roz didn't know what to say. It was hard to pick a fight with someone who didn't want to fight back. Ozzie just refused to believe that she didn't want to spend all her free time with him.

"Oh, Ozzie," she moaned. "Just for once will you leave me alone?"

They had reached the doors, side by side, of the two-family house where they both lived.

"How can I leave you alone?" asked Ozzie as he opened the door to his home. "Don't forget, I'm your uncle!"

2
Roz's Family

"Is that true?" asked Brie as the two girls entered Roz's house.

"Is what true?" asked Roz. But she knew what Brie wanted to know.

"That little kid, Ozzie, who spilled the pennies—is he your uncle?"

"Yeah," Roz mumbled.

"But that's impossible! He's much too young to be an uncle."

"What's impossible?" asked Roz's mother, coming to greet the girls.

Even though Mrs. Sasser was older than Ozzie, you could immediately see a resemblance. She had all the same freckles that Ozzie had.

"Mom, this is Brie," said Roz, introducing her classmate. "She just met Ozzie. And as usual he was up to his old tricks. Do you know what he did today? He spilled a thousand pennies in the bus on the way home. There was practically a riot."

Brie giggled. "It was kind of funny, actually," she said.

Mrs. Sasser smiled at the girls. "That's Ozzie for you," she said.

"How can he be Roz's uncle?" Brie wanted to know. "What does that make him to you?" she asked Roz's mother.

"He's my brother. Or actually, he's my half brother. We have the same mother," Mrs. Sasser explained. "Ozzie's and my mother is Roz's grandmother. My mother was widowed when I was a kid, and she remarried just around the same time that I married Roz's father. So her husband, George, is Ozzie's father; he's my stepfather; and he's Roz's step-grandfather."

"If Ozzie is your half brother, he should be my half uncle," said Roz. "A half uncle should bother me half as much as Ozzie does."

15

"Oh, Roz," said her mother. "Ozzie's not so bad. And now that we live so near, it's almost as if you have a brother—except that he has different parents."

"I'd rather have my own real brother," said Roz. "Or else a sister."

"It sounds awfully complicated to me," said Brie. "I have grown-up uncles and aunts and I have a little whole brother."

"That's a normal family," said Roz.

Mrs. Sasser reached out her hand and felt Roz's forehead. "You feel normal to me," she said. "Since you don't have a fever, maybe you and Brie would like to have a snack. There's a bag of cookies on the counter. And help yourself to milk or juice from the fridge. I'll be working in the living room if you need me."

Roz and Brie went into the kitchen.

"What's your mom doing in the living room?" asked Brie. "Is she cleaning?"

"Cleaning?" scoffed Roz. "She's doing her homework for school."

"School? You mean she still goes to school?" asked Brie.

"I told you my family's not normal,"

sighed Roz. "My mother got married while she was going to college, but when I was born, she stopped going to school. Then a few years ago, she went back to finish college. And now she just got a teaching fellowship at the university, so she can become a doctor. She's not learning how to cure anybody or anything. My mother is going to become a doctor of literature."

"What's that?" asked Brie.

"Books," said Roz. "My mother reads loads of books, more than anyone you ever saw. And she especially likes books by a woman named Virginia Woolf. That's going to be the subject for her dissertation."

"What's that?" asked Brie.

"It's like writing a long, long, long book report," Roz explained. "But instead of reading just one book, you write it after you've read dozens and dozens of books."

Roz opened the bag of chocolate-chip cookies and offered it to Brie. Then she took one for herself.

"Milk or juice?" Roz asked Brie.

Both girls had glasses of milk.

"What does your father do?" asked Brie. "Does he go to school, too?"

"Yes," said Roz. Then she giggled. "That's because he works in a school. He teaches English at the high school."

"Which school do you like better, your old school or the one we're going to now?" asked Brie.

"I miss my friends from my old school," Roz admitted. "But if you're going to be my friend, I guess I'll start liking my new school a whole lot more."

"How come you moved here?" asked Brie.

"My grandparents' tenants moved out of this part of the house during the summer. So they suggested we move in because it's so close to the university where my mother is studying."

Suddenly Brie let out a shriek and knocked over her glass of milk.

"What's the matter?" asked Roz, startled.

Brie pointed to the kitchen window and started giggling. "Look," she said. "He scared me."

Roz looked and saw Ozzie's squashed

nose pressed against the glass window as he peered in at them. It was the first time she had brought a friend home from school. She wondered if Ozzie was planning to act like this every time she didn't include him in her activities.

Roz opened the window. "Can't we have any privacy?" she yelled at Ozzie.

"I just wondered what you were doing," said Ozzie.

"We're eating cookies," said Roz.

"And spilling milk," added Brie, laughing. She brought the bag of cookies over to the window and held it out. "Do you want one?"

Ozzie reached in and took a cookie. "Thanks," he said. "Can I come inside?"

"No!" said Roz. "Now get lost." She brought the window down with a bang and pulled the window shade down, too, hoping that would discourage Ozzie.

Ozzie began tapping on the pane of glass.

"Just ignore him," Roz instructed Brie. "Do you want some more milk?" she asked as she wiped up the milk that Brie had spilled on the table. Some of the milk was dripping down one of the table legs and onto the floor.

Ozzie kept tapping on the window.

"Aren't you going to ask him what he wants?" said Brie.

"I know what he wants," said Roz. "He wants to bother us. I didn't mind him so much when we didn't live next door to each other and I only saw him once in a while. But now that I see him every day, I've discovered he can be a real pain. Don't you just hate boys?"

"Some boys," Brie agreed. "But not all of them. Some boys are nice. I like to help take care of my brother. He's only a baby. He's eighteen months."

"I bet it's fun to have a baby to play with," said Roz. She bit into another cookie. Then she said, "Do you like Paul Olson?" It was a question she had been dying to ask her classmate.

"Oh, no," said Brie, shaking her head vigorously. But her face flushed as she answered, and Roz thought that perhaps Brie wasn't telling the truth.

"I think he likes you," Roz said.

"Really? He *is* kind of cute."

"He says funny things," said Roz. "Remember when Mrs. Corey said we each had to pick two states to give reports on, and he called out Rhode Island and Connecticut?"

"And Mrs. Corey said, 'Paul, are you interested in New England?' and he said, 'No. Those are just about the two smallest states of all, so I won't have to write so much.'"

"It shows he's smart, even if he is lazy," said Roz. "I don't know which states are big and which ones are small."

"Me neither," said Brie. "But then Mrs. Corey said, 'Paul, you can have Rhode Island and Alaska. It will make a good contrast.'"

"She could have made him do Alaska and Texas," said Roz. "Even I know they are the biggest states of all."

"I have Mississippi and Wyoming," said Brie, removing the two books she had borrowed from the school library from her backpack.

"I have Florida and West Virginia," said Roz. "Have you ever been to any of these places?"

22

"Nope," said Brie. "Have you?"

"No."

They had to read about their states and prepare travel brochures to tell their classmates about the most important facts and sights of interest in each area. Luckily, they had three weeks. It would take a long time to draw the maps and look up all the information.

The tapping on the window had stopped. Thank goodness Ozzie had gone away at last, Roz thought as she turned the pages in the book about Florida. She wondered if Ozzie was walking Samantha.

"I'll be right back," Roz told Brie. She went into the living room to speak to her mother. Mrs. Sasser was surrounded by books.

"Can Brie have supper here?" asked Roz.

"Honey, don't forget this is Tuesday," said Mrs. Sasser. Tuesday night was microwave night. Mrs. Sasser taught a class at the university every Tuesday, and Roz and her father each selected a dinner from the freezer.

"There are lots of things in the freezer,"

said Mrs. Sasser. "But maybe you'd rather have Brie stay some evening when we're cooking a real meal."

"I'll ask her," said Roz.

"Do you want to stay and have supper with me?" Roz asked Brie hopefully.

"What are you having tonight?"

"Do you like chicken?" asked Roz. "We have a lot of chicken."

"Oh, sure," said Brie. "I love chicken."

"You can take your pick," said Roz as she opened the freezer door. She began reading the names off the packages stored inside. "Here's chicken enchilada, chicken marsala, chicken biryani, chicken tika makhanwala. . . ."

"Those sound kind of strange," said Brie. "I like just plain chicken chicken."

"My mother buys these frozen dinners that we can heat up in the microwave on nights when she isn't home. She and my father like to try new kinds of meals. I think my father said the chicken biryani and the chicken tika makhanwala are from India. Anyhow, they're not too bad if you like spicy food. I kind of like them."

24

"Well, I just remembered that I can't stay today," said Brie. "But maybe sometime you can come to my house for dinner instead. My mother cooks ordinary American food. You'd probably like it."

Roz was disappointed, but she didn't let it show.

Brie went to the phone to call her mother for a ride, and the girls worked on their homework for a while longer.

"I'll see you in school tomorrow," Brie said when she heard the honking of a car horn outside on the street.

"Okay," said Roz. She stood in the doorway and waved as Brie drove off with her mother.

The honking horn had brought Ozzie and his mother to the door, too.

"Hi, Roz, honey," said her grandmother, giving her a hug. "What are you up to?"

"Not much," said Roz. "I was doing my homework with a girl from my class."

"How would you like to have supper with us?" her grandmother offered. "There's a fresh pot of chicken vegetable soup on the stove."

"Come on, Roz. Say yes!" said Ozzie.

Roz thought about the frozen dinners in the freezer. She couldn't blame Brie for leaving. She didn't feel like eating chicken tika makhanwala either.

"Okay," she said. "I'll tell Mom."

"I know this is her teaching night. And tell your father he's invited for supper, too."

Roz went back into the house to talk with her mother. "Grandma invited Dad and me to have supper with her," she said.

"Lucky you," said Mrs. Sasser. She was organizing her books and papers before she went off to teach her class.

Suddenly Roz remembered that she had forgotten to point out Brie's pierced ears to her mother. The afternoon had not gone as she had planned. It was Ozzie's fault. If they hadn't been talking about him when they entered the house, she would have remembered. He really was a pain.

Nevertheless, twenty minutes later, she was sitting across the table from that penny-spilling, window-tapping, riddle-asking nuisance, her uncle Ozzie.

26

3

Good Soup & Bad Jokes

"What a treat!" said Roz's father as he took the first spoonful of chicken vegetable soup from his bowl. He smiled across the table at his daughter. "This is our lucky night, Roz."

Roz stirred her soup. Even though she found Ozzie a pain, she loved both her grandparents. So she guessed her father was right. She was lucky to be sitting here for supper.

The thing that Roz liked best about her grandmother's soup was that it wasn't watery like most soups. There were pieces of chicken, alphabet noodles, and bits of to-

27

mato, as well as carrots and celery and onions and corn and peas and beans.

"You make the best soup in the whole world," Roz told her grandmother when she finished chewing her first mouthful.

"I'm glad you like it," Mrs. Sims said. "But I have a surprise for you. I didn't make it."

"It came out of a can?" asked Roz in amazement. That was a surprise, but it was good news, too. If canned soup was so delicious, she would insist her mother buy this brand the next time she went shopping.

"Ozzie made it," said Roz's grandmother.

"Ozzie? I don't believe it. How could he make it?" asked Roz. "He's just a little kid. He's younger than me and I can't make soup."

"You'd be amazed what little kids can do. Right, Ozzie?" Mrs. Sims said.

"Well, Mom told me what to do. First I cut up all the vegetables. Then I threw them into the pot of water," said Ozzie. "It was easy—except for cutting up the carrots. That was the only hard part." He thought for a minute. "And the onions. They make you cry even if you're feeling happy."

Roz turned to her grandfather. "Do you believe that Ozzie made this soup?"

Roz's grandfather took a large spoonful of soup and ate it slowly. Then he nodded his head. "Yes," he said. "Ozzie made it."

"Does it taste that different tonight?" asked Roz.

Roz's grandfather took still another spoonful of soup. After he chewed it up and swallowed he said, "It tastes the same as always, but when I came home from work I saw Ozzie cutting up the vegetables and stirring the things in the pot. So I guess that makes me a witness. Ozzie did make it." He winked at Ozzie.

"Anytime you want to come cook with Ozzie and me, just come right into the kitchen," offered Roz's grandmother. "I'll be glad to teach you."

"We could do it tomorrow," suggested Ozzie eagerly. "What are we going to make tomorrow?" he asked his mother.

"Meatloaf," said his mother.

Roz knew their meatloaf would be better than chicken tika makhanwala.

"Great," said Ozzie.

"I have a Girl Scout meeting tomorrow," said Roz. "I won't be coming home from school until late." One of the first things Roz had done after they moved was to join the local troop. She had been a Girl Scout in her old town, too.

"It doesn't have to be tomorrow," said her grandmother. "My offer is open. Any day. Any time."

"Take her up on it," urged Roz's father. "Maybe I'll come over for a lesson or two myself, if I'm invited."

"Of course you're invited, Steve," Roz's grandmother told him.

"Did you teach my mom to cook when she was Ozzie's age?" Roz wanted to know.

"Joan?" asked Mrs. Sims, referring to her daughter. "I certainly did. In those days, I was going to school, just like she is now. After Joan's father died, I went back to school and got a nursing degree. When I came in from the hospital in the late afternoon, Joan would have supper on the table waiting for me."

"Well, she doesn't do very much cooking now, does she, Dad?" said Roz.

"It's hard to be a mother and go to school and cook elaborate meals, too," said Mrs. Sims. "I remember those days only too well."

"I wouldn't say we're starving," said Roz's father. "Some nights we have microwave dinners and some nights I do the cooking."

"Oh, Dad," said Roz. "You only know how to cook one thing."

"But I make it better than anyone else in the world," said Mr. Sasser proudly.

Somewhere, somehow, Roz's father had learned to make very good sauce for spaghetti. And at least once a week, that's what they had for supper.

"When I married your grandmother, I didn't even know she knew how to cook," said Roz's grandfather. "But I thought it would be handy to live with a nurse during my old age."

"You're not old," said Roz. "At least not so very old." She knew that her grandfather, like her grandmother, had been married before. He was a widower when he met and married Roz's grandmother. He had never had any children before Ozzie. Roz's mother had told her that when Ozzie was born her grandfather was beside himself with joy. He hadn't expected to become a father at his age.

"Ozzie keeps me young," said Roz's grandfather.

Ozzie beamed with pride. "I've got some new riddles," he notified the people sitting around the table. "Don't tell them the answers," he instructed Roz.

"He bothered Brie and me with his silly old riddles this afternoon," Roz complained.

"Well, I bet Brie liked them, even if you didn't," said Ozzie.

"Brie?" asked Mr. Sasser.

"She's my friend from school. She came to visit me, but Ozzie was a nuisance. He banged on the window and bothered us. I don't know when he had time to cook anything, he was so busy being a pest."

"Brie?" said Mr. Sasser again. "That's a

kind of cheese. Where did you find a girl named after a cheese?"

Roz looked surprised. "I didn't know that," she said. "I think Brie's a very pretty name," she added. Then she giggled.

"Guess what her brother is named," she said.

"Cheddar?" shouted Ozzie.

"Graham. Like in graham crackers," said Roz.

"It's like a riddle," said Roz's grand-mother.

"Let's hear your riddles, Ozzie," said her grandfather.

"Yes. Let's see if you're going to stump us as you usually do," said Roz's father.

Roz braced herself to listen to Ozzie's corny riddles again. Sure enough, he asked about the duck crossing the road. Next he asked about the dinosaur. None of the adults sitting at the table knew the answers. Then Ozzie came up with another stupid riddle. It was not one he had asked Brie that afternoon.

"Do you know why the chicken crossed

the road? To get the Chinese newspaper," Ozzie announced. "Do you get it?"

"No," admitted Roz's father.

"Neither do I," said Ozzie. "I get the *Daily Herald.*"

Roz groaned, but her father and grandfather both laughed.

"Listen," said Roz's grandfather. "Did you people hear about the bad accident that happened on the henway?"

"Henway? What's a henway?" asked Roz's grandmother.

"Oh, about five to six pounds," Roz's grandfather answered.

There was a moment of silence. Then Ozzie began laughing with delight. "Oh, that's great. I'll tell that one at school tomorrow."

As if things weren't bad enough, Roz thought to herself. Now her grandfather was supplying Ozzie with still more corny riddles to torment her with.

Mrs. Sims removed the empty soup bowls from the table and put out a large bowl of homemade applesauce.

"Did Ozzie make this?" asked Roz.

"No. But he made these," said her grandmother. She placed a plate of oatmeal cookies on the table.

After the supper dishes were cleared away, everyone went into the living room. Some evenings Roz's father played catch outside with Roz and Ozzie. Lately he was teaching them how to throw and catch a football. But this evening it had begun to rain, so they couldn't go out and play.

"I guess I'd better excuse myself," Mr. Sasser said. "I have a ton of papers to grade this evening." He gave his mother-in-law a kiss. "Thanks for the wonderful meal."

"After I teach you to cook, I'll come have dinner in your place," said Mrs. Sims.

Roz's grandmother took up her needles and began to knit. Roz had planned to leave with her father, but she loved watching her grandmother's fingers move so quickly as she knit. The wool was wrapped around one finger and the stitches slid from one needle to another. It was almost like magic.

"What are you making?" she asked.

36

"A sweater for your grandfather."

"It's a surprise for my birthday," said Roz's grandfather, looking up from his newspaper.

"It can't be a surprise if you watch her making it," said Roz.

"Oh," said her grandfather. "That's a surprise."

"Is it hard to knit?" asked Roz.

"It can't be hard, because I've seen her knitting and watching TV at the same time," said Ozzie. "She can do it without looking."

"Without looking at the TV?" asked Roz.

"No, silly. Without looking at the knitting."

"Will you teach me how to knit?" asked Roz.

"Sure," said her grandmother. "Let me finish this row of stitches, and I'll find some needles for you to use. Or I could teach you how to crochet. You only need one crochet needle, and it might be easier to begin with crocheting."

"Okay," agreed Roz. She had often admired her grandmother's crocheting, too.

"I want to learn, too," said Ozzie.

"Boys don't crochet or knit," said Roz.

"Why not?" asked Ozzie. "I can do it if I want to."

"Grandpa doesn't crochet or knit."

"I'm not a boy," said Roz's grandfather. "But I suppose I could learn how to do those things if I wanted to. The problem is, I don't want to."

"But I do," said Ozzie with determination.

Roz wasn't sure she wanted to learn if Ozzie was going to be doing it, too.

"Here," said her grandmother. "I have some leftover wool from that sweater I made you for your birthday last year. And here are needles for both of you." Mrs. Sims put a crochet hook in Roz's hand. "Now, this is the way you hold it," she instructed. "I'll teach you how to make a chain. If you can do that, you can crochet anything."

At first, it wasn't easy at all. The crochet hook kept slipping out of Roz's hand, and the loops of wool slipped off the needle.

Roz looked to see how Ozzie was making out.

Ozzie had the wool wrapped around his finger and an intense expression on his face. But when he looked up from his crocheting and saw Roz looking at him, he grinned at her.

"This is fun," he said. "But cooking is easier."

"Crocheting lasts longer," said his mother.

"Look how long my chain is," said Roz.

"Let's have a race to see who can make the longest chain," suggested Ozzie.

"If you want to do a good job and make all your stitches the same size, don't race. Just do it for pleasure. After a while, you'll be able to crochet and watch television at the same time, just like me," said her grandmother.

"What can I make?" asked Roz. Her chain was about a foot long, but it didn't look like much.

"After you practice a bit, you could make a scarf for the winter."

"Maybe I'll make one for Grandpa as a surprise," said Roz.

"If you finish it, it will be a surprise," said her grandfather, winking at her.

"Of course I'll finish it. You'll see," said Roz.

She was surprised when her grand-mother told her it was almost eight-thirty. It was time for her to go home and get ready for bed.

Roz gave her grandmother and her grandfather good-night kisses.

"I'll see you in the morning," said Ozzie, looking up from his crocheting.

Even though he followed her to school and home again, Roz knew Ozzie didn't ex-pect or want a good-night kiss. She also knew he wouldn't go to bed until he was sure his crocheted chain was a lot longer than hers. So she stuck her tongue out at him instead.

"Good night, Uncle Ozzie," she said.

4

Fair Rosalind

Every morning before she left for school, Roz had a bowl of instant oatmeal. And every morning, she counted out exactly fifteen raisins to sprinkle over her cereal. Fifteen was the perfect number. She had tried fourteen and she had tried sixteen. But for some reason, her oatmeal tasted best with fifteen raisins.

This morning as Roz ate her cereal, she thought once again about her wish to get her ears pierced. It seemed as if just about every girl in the fourth grade in her new school had pierced ears. And almost every girl in Roz's new Scout troop wore earrings,

41

too. Roz had been wanting to do it for a long time, and she didn't want to wait until she got any older.

"I want to get my ears pierced now," she announced to her parents.

"Now?" said her father, who was gathering up his books and papers before leaving for the high school. "It's time to go to school."

"Oh, Dad. You know I don't mean *now*, now. I mean now, this week," said Roz.

"I never wanted to," said her mother. "Why do you? You might get infections in your earlobes."

"I asked Grandma about that," said Roz. The last time she had asked about getting her ears pierced, her mother had brought up the possibility of infections, too. "Grandma said if you put alcohol on your earlobes for the first couple of weeks, there won't be any problem. And she's a nurse, so she should know."

Roz turned to her father for support. "All the girls I know have pierced ears. It makes them look pretty," said Roz. "Please."

42

Instead of giving an opinion about earrings, Mr. Sasser began to recite:

"From the east to western Ind,
No jewel is like Rosalind.
Her worth, being mounted on the wind,
Through all the world bears Rosalind.
All the pictures fairest lin'd
Are but black to Rosalind.
Let no face be kept in mind
But the fair of Rosalind."

"What's that?" asked Roz. Her father often quoted poetry to her.

"A description of the lovely Rosalind from Shakespeare's play *As You Like It*. My third-year English honors class is reading it just now, as a matter of fact. I've told you that when your mother and I were picking out girls' names before you were born, one of the reasons I argued for 'Rosalind' was because of that play. Of course, I couldn't have known that we'd almost never call you anything but Roz."

"If the Rosalind in the play was so pretty,

it must be because her ears were pierced," said Roz confidently.

"Actually, when the play was performed in the seventeenth century, the role of Rosalind was played by a young man."

"Lots of men wear earrings these days," said Roz, undaunted. "I bet Virginia Woolf had her ears pierced, too," she said, appealing to her mother again.

"To tell the truth, that's one piece of information I haven't uncovered in my research," said Mrs. Sasser. Then she added, "All right. They're your ears. If you want to do it, it's okay with me. One of these days I'll take you to Forbes Department Store. They do it at the jewelry counter there."

"When? When?" nagged Roz. Having convinced her mother at last, she was impatient to get her ears pierced at once.

"What's the rush? Maybe we'll do it for your birthday next month."

"Oh, no. I don't want to wait that long," Roz protested.

"Well, I'm awfully busy right now. You know I have to hand in the outline for my dissertation by the end of the month," said Mrs. Sasser.

Roz sighed.

"I could take you tomorrow afternoon when I get home from work," offered Roz's father.

"Oh, super!" shouted Roz. She gave each of her parents a big hug.

What was not super was that when the time came Ozzie rode along with them. That was bad. Ozzie could be such a pain in the neck. But two days a week, Roz's grandmother still worked at the hospital. And as this was one of those days, Ozzie was expected to hang around with Roz.

"I wish Ozzie didn't have to come along," Roz had grumbled to her father before Ozzie came out of his house and into the car.

"Why not?"

"He always comes everywhere with us these days," Roz complained.

"Unless you're going somewhere with him," Mr. Sasser reminded his daughter. "You didn't complain when your grandfather took both of you to the movies last Saturday. And you didn't complain when your grandparents took the two of you to play miniature golf the weekend before."

"That's different," said Roz.

"No, it's not," Mr. Sasser insisted.

The other thing that wasn't super about getting one's ears pierced was that it might hurt. That was a problem that worried Roz. And what was worse was having two ears. Suppose she got a hole in one ear and then was afraid to get the second hole. Wouldn't she look weird with only one earring? She'd look like the clerk at the checkout counter of the supermarket who had only one earring. And he was a man.

"It can't hurt very much," said Roz's father, guessing his daughter's thoughts. "If it hurt, no one would ever get it done."

"You're pretty as you are," said Ozzie. "If I were you, I wouldn't have my ears pierced." He rubbed his own earlobes thoughtfully.

"They're having a sale on sport shirts," said Mr. Sasser. "I want to pick up a couple.

46

If you change your mind, I'll buy my shirts and we'll just come back home."

So there they were—Roz and Ozzie and Mr. Sasser in Forbes Department Store.

"Why don't you ride up and down on the escalator?" Roz suggested to Ozzie as they approached the jewelry counter on the ground floor. "You like to do that." In fact, the two of them had ridden up and down together just a couple of weeks ago when Roz's grandmother was buying new sheets and pillowcases in this same store.

"I want to watch," Ozzie insisted. That was exactly what Roz knew he was going to say.

There was only one saleswoman at the jewelry counter, and she was busy helping a customer.

"What kind of earrings are you going to get?" asked Ozzie.

Roz studied the display. There were earrings shaped like hearts and there were earrings shaped like stars. There were also tiny teddy bears, tiny mushrooms, tiny seashells, and tiny leaves. There were plain round earrings of gold or silver, and there were tiny pearl earrings, too. It was a hard decision. Roz wished Brie was with her to help her pick out the best ones.

The other customer picked up her purchase and walked away. The saleswoman came over toward Mr. Sasser. "Can I help you?" she asked.

"My daughter wants to get her ears pierced," said Roz's father.

"Okay," said the woman. "Let her pick out a pair of earrings and I'll insert them in her ears."

The woman bent under the counter and pulled out a bottle of rubbing alcohol and a box of cotton. "You'll have to wipe your earlobes with alcohol every morning and every evening for the next two weeks to prevent infection," she told Roz.

Roz nodded and wrinkled her nose. The open bottle of alcohol had a familiar smell. It was like being in a doctor's office.

"I'm not sure," said Roz softly, meaning she wasn't sure she wanted to go ahead with this operation.

"The gold stars are very popular with girls your age," said the saleswoman. She obviously thought Roz wasn't sure which earrings to get.

"Are you getting scared?" asked Ozzie. "I wouldn't want anyone to make holes in my ears."

"I'm not scared," said Roz. "But maybe I should wait until another day so I pick out the right earrings."

"Well, you won't be wearing the same ones forever," laughed the saleswoman. "Whichever ones you don't pick today, you can buy next time."

"Let's go upstairs and get my shirts," suggested Mr. Sasser. "We can stop back down here before we leave the store. It will give you a little more time to make up your mind."

Roz smiled at her father with relief. "That's a good idea," she said. She wanted to get away from the jewelry counter and the saleswoman and the smell of the rubbing alcohol.

The woman screwed the top back on the

alcohol bottle and replaced it under the counter.

"She's scared," Ozzie told the saleslady.

"Oh, I'm sure your sister isn't frightened. Ear piercing hardly hurts at all."

"I'm not his sister," said Roz. As she spoke she thought about what the woman had just said. *Hardly hurts at all.* That meant that it must hurt at least a little.

"I'm her uncle," said Ozzie.

"Uncle!" gasped the woman. "Well, that *is* a surprise."

Roz glared at Ozzie. Why did he always have to go around announcing the fact?

The three of them took the escalator upstairs to men's sportswear. It took Mr. Sasser only a couple of minutes to pick out his shirts—two for the price of one. He selected a red checked shirt and a blue plaid one.

"Earrings are two for the price of one, too," said Ozzie. "But Roz is scared. She isn't going to get her ears pierced today."

"I am so," said Roz. There was no way she was going to let Ozzie go to school to-

50

morrow and tell everyone on the bus that she had chickened out. It would become one of his chicken riddles. *Why did Roz cross the road? Because she was too chicken to get her ears pierced.*

"Let's go back to the jewelry department right now," Roz said.

Mr. Sasser paid for his shirts and they went down the escalator and back to the jewelry counter.

"You're back?" said the saleswoman, looking surprised.

"I want the heart earrings," said Roz firmly.

"Fine," said the woman. She took a pair of tiny gold hearts and placed them on the counter. Then she reached under the counter again for the alcohol and the cotton. She put some alcohol on a small piece of cotton and rubbed each of Roz's ears. It felt cold, but it didn't hurt.

Next she took a ballpoint pen that was in the breast pocket of her smock and touched each of Roz's ears with it.

"What's that for?" asked Ozzie suspiciously. He reached out and took Roz's hand.

"I have to mark where to make the holes," said the woman. "We want them to be balanced. Each hole should be in exactly the same part of the earlobe."

Roz held on to Ozzie's hand as she watched the woman's every movement. It might be babyish, but it felt comforting to have someone holding her hand. Mr. Sasser had moved along the counter and was examining some of the other jewelry that was on display.

Bending again under the counter, the saleswoman brought up something that looked like a stapler. She seemed to be adjusting it, and then she held it near Roz's right ear. "Hold still," she said, and suddenly Roz felt the sensation of having her earlobe pinched. She squeezed Ozzie's hand and he squeezed back. The woman moved the stapler to the left ear and pinched that lobe, too.

"All right," she said, stepping back from Roz.

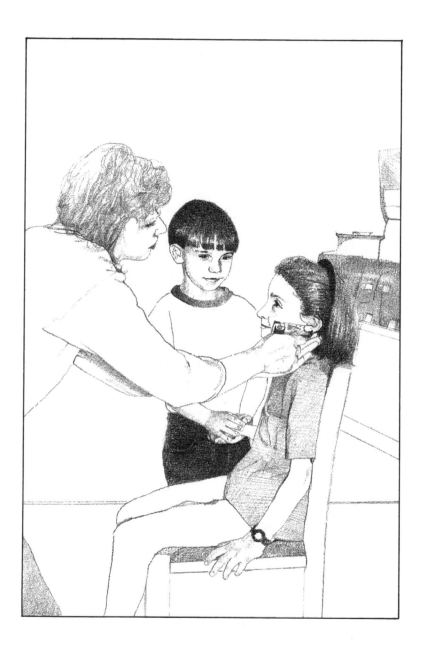

"When are you going to pierce my ears?" asked Roz.

"I already did. You're all done!" said the woman. She held a mirror out to Roz so that she could see for herself.

Roz dropped Ozzie's hand and took the mirror. There she was, just as before, but now there was a tiny gold heart in each ear.

"You look beautiful!" said Ozzie.

Roz stared at herself with disbelief. It really hadn't hurt at all. And to think she almost hadn't gone through with it. In fact, she realized, if she hadn't been afraid that Ozzie would tell everyone at school, she would have gone home with her ears unpierced. She remembered it had felt comforting to hold on to his hand, too. It was really a good thing that her uncle had come along, after all.

Roz smiled at Ozzie.

She smiled all the way home in the car. And her father again recited Shakespeare's poetry:

"From the east to western Ind,
No jewel is like Rosalind. . . ."

5

Ozzie Is a Thief

It was Monday. Roz didn't have a Girl Scout meeting. She didn't have a friend coming home from school with her. And no one had invited her over. So when the school bus stopped at the corner of Kinkade and Corn, she had no other choice. Roz got off the bus followed as always by Ozzie.

"What are we going to do this afternoon?" he asked.

"I don't know what *you're* going to do, but it has nothing to do with me!" Roz yelled. She got so tired of having Ozzie following her all the time.

"I am your uncle," said Ozzie. He knew

it annoyed her, so he repeated the fact often.

"I wish I had a real grown-up uncle like other people. Brie told me today about hers. He came to visit over the weekend. He brought her a present and took her for a ride in his new sports car. That's the way uncles are supposed to be. They're supposed to buy you presents and take you places. They're not supposed to be little, like you."

"When I get old enough to buy a car, I'll take you for a ride," offered Ozzie.

"Well, I'm older, so I'll have a car first," said Roz. It was a small consolation.

When they reached the house, Roz quickly said good-bye to Ozzie and rushed inside before he could begin further discussion about what they could do together. Some days that worked. Today was not such a day. Within ten minutes of Roz's entering the house, dropping her backpack, and peeking in on her mother, who was sitting at the computer entering data about Virginia Woolf, there was a knock on the door.

"Will you come with me to Bargain World?" asked Ozzie when Roz opened the door. "My mom needs some stuff, and she said I could go for her if you'll come along with me. Okay? So let's go."

Roz thought of the alternatives. She could read her library book. She could do her homework. She could . . . She couldn't think of anything else she could do.

"All right," she agreed. "What do you have to buy?"

"My mom needs a spool of black thread and a box of business envelopes," said Ozzie. "Hey, Joan," he called to Roz's mother. "Do you need anything at Bargain World?"

After all these years, it still seemed weird to Roz to hear Ozzie call her parents by their first names. Kids always called adults Mr. or Mrs. or Aunt or Uncle. Whenever she brought someone home from school, they always called her mother Mrs. Sasser. But Mrs. Sasser was Ozzie's sister, so he just called her Joan.

"Hi, Ozzie," Roz's mother called out, not

taking her eyes from the computer screen. "I need about six months of peace and quiet. I don't think you'll find that at Bargain World."

Peace and quiet were almost the only things you couldn't find at the store. It was a large discount store with many, many counters selling items at low prices. In addition to thread, there were sewing patterns and fabric remnants. There was also wool and knitting needles and crochet hooks. In addition to business envelopes, there were padded mailing envelopes and large manila envelopes and file folders. There were pads of paper and stationery and paper clips and scissors and many kinds of tape. There was an aisle with boxes of imported cookies and crackers. There was another area of the store where you could buy underwear and sunglasses and nonprescription drugs and shampoo and deodorant. You couldn't buy meat and vegetables at Bargain World. And you couldn't find peace and quiet, because at any hour that you visited, the aisles were always filled with people looking for things to buy.

The store was just a short walk from Roz's home, and she liked to go there. No matter how many times she had walked up and down the aisles since moving to this neighborhood, she always discovered something brand-new that she hadn't seen the time before. One week they were selling paperback books—two for a dollar. Another time they had neat canvas shoes imported from China. Roz wondered what she and Ozzie would find today.

She watched as Ozzie picked out the spool of black thread that his mother wanted. He turned in the direction of the stationery counter.

"Let's just look around on our own," Ozzie suggested suddenly. "We can meet at the door at four-thirty and walk home together."

Roz wondered if Ozzie was sick. He never wanted to walk around the store on his own. She had been here with him before, and he always insisted on following after her. Maybe he is changing, she thought incredulously.

Roz stood still for a moment as a mother

with a young child pushed past her. She had to decide where to look first. Should she look at the cookie area? Sometimes they gave out free samples. She could study the choices of wool. Her grandmother said she was getting along just fine with her crocheting so maybe she should pick out some wool to begin work on a scarf for the winter. Or maybe she should look and see if there was something totally new on display today.

Roz wondered what Ozzie was looking at. She glanced about and thought she saw him down the next aisle. What was over there? She walked toward Ozzie. He looked up, and as he saw her he slipped something from the counter into his pocket. Roz stopped short. She couldn't have imagined it. Ozzie had just stolen something off the counter. It was hard to believe—Roz's uncle Ozzie was a thief.

"Hey, Ozzie," said Roz.

Those parts of the skin on Ozzie's face that weren't covered with freckles became bright red. That was certainly proof he was feeling guilty about something.

"What do you want?" asked Ozzie. His left hand was holding the spool of thread, and his right hand was in his pocket. "Why aren't you looking around?"

"I'm looking, but I'm not stealing," Roz hissed into Ozzie's ear.

"Of course you're not stealing," said Ozzie. He pushed Roz away from the section where he had been standing. "Some kid at school said he heard they were going to have goldfish and turtles for sale here. I can't find them. Did you see them?"

"Goldfish?" asked Roz. "I saw some cans of tuna fish. What do you have in your pocket, Ozzie?"

"My hand," said her uncle, pulling it out of his pocket.

"Okay. I know your hand was in your pocket. What else is in there?"

"My pennies," said Ozzie. "How come you're so nosy about my pocket all of a sudden? I never ask you what's in your pockets."

"Ozzie. You may be my uncle, but I'm older than you. And if you don't take out

61

the thing that you stole from your pocket, I'm going to, to, to . . ." Roz wondered what she would do. She didn't want to tell the store manager about Ozzie. Ozzie would get in big trouble if anyone found out he had been stealing. She wondered if he had done it before. Maybe he had done it lots of times, and this was the first time she had caught him in the act.

"You're crazy," said Ozzie. "I didn't steal anything."

"I saw you with my own eyes," said Roz. "I have twenty-twenty vision, and I know what I saw."

"Well, I know what I did and what I didn't do," said Ozzie. "Besides," he said, "I thought we were going to meet at the door at four-thirty. How come you're following me all around the store?"

"Me following you?" Roz shouted at her uncle. Up until now she had been whispering so no one would hear what she had to say about Ozzie stealing. But really, it was too much. "You're always following me. And for once I turn around to look at you, and I discover you're a thief. A criminal. You're going to wind up in jail."

A few people stopped to watch and listen. Ozzie's freckled face turned red again. He tried to smile at the onlookers.

Roz turned red when she noticed their audience, too. "This is a private discussion," she said to the woman standing nearest her, who was looking from Roz to Ozzie and back again. Roz leaned over and whispered into Ozzie's ear, "Put it back and let's get out of here."

"Leave me alone, Roz," Ozzie whined.

"Not until you take whatever you have out of your pocket," Roz retorted.

"You better put it back, kid," said an older woman who had been standing nearby and listening to Roz and Ozzie.

"I didn't steal anything," Ozzie protested again.

"Then let me see what's in your pocket," said Roz. "Then I'll believe you."

"I can't," said Ozzie.

"See," said Roz, turning to the woman. "My uncle is a thief." She didn't know why, but tears began to slide down her cheeks.

"You have an uncle who is a thief, too?" inquired the woman. "That *is* a shame. I've heard that the tendency to a life of crime is often passed from one generation to the next."

Roz found a tissue in the pocket of her sweater and blew her nose.

"It's not too late for your brother to change his ways," the woman assured Roz. Then she turned and walked away.

"He's not my brother," Roz called after the woman.

"I'm not stealing anything," Ozzie said angrily. "I was trying to secretly buy you a present, but now you've made everybody in the store think I'm a criminal."

"A present?" said Roz. "I don't believe it."

"Why would I want these?" asked Ozzie. He pulled a small black card from his pocket. Attached to the card was a pair of small enameled earrings. They were tiny red stars.

"Do you have money to pay for them?" Roz asked Ozzie anxiously.

"Of course," said Ozzie.

Roz didn't say anything more. She felt amazingly stupid.

Afterward, Roz didn't know which was more embarrassing. Was it accusing her uncle of stealing when he was trying to buy her a surprise gift? Or was it standing at the checkout counter and waiting while Ozzie Sims counted out 179 pennies from his pockets to pay for the present?

"Thank goodness you didn't pick out a more expensive item," said a woman who was standing behind Ozzie on the checkout line.

"I have lots more pennies at home," Ozzie assured her.

"I'm sure you do," said the woman. "But I don't have a week to wait on this line while you count them out."

Nevertheless, the cashier took the pennies and the time delay in stride. "We can always use pennies," she said as she re-counted the little piles of coins that Ozzie made on the counter.

"Don't you remember? You said that un-cles were supposed to give gifts to their

66

nieces," Ozzie reminded Roz as they walked home together. Ozzie was holding a paper bag with the box of business envelopes and the spool of black thread for his mother. Roz was carrying the little card with the tiny earrings attached to it.

"I wanted it to be a surprise," said Ozzie.

"Don't worry," said Roz. "It was."

6

Roz's Birthday

At Roz's old school, one day each month was set aside to celebrate all the birthdays of that month. Roz had discovered there was a different tradition at her new school. Students celebrating their birthdays brought cookies or cupcakes as a treat for their classmates on the day of the event.

As Roz's ninth birthday approached, she began planning for this. A girl named Jessica in her class had brought cupcakes on the last Monday in September. A boy named Brian had brought homemade chocolate-chip cookies, two for each person in the class. The cookies were good, but Roz decided that cupcakes were more like a little party.

"Everyone brings things their mother baked," said Roz to her mother. "Will you bake cupcakes?"

"Oh, honey. I don't have time for that," complained Mrs. Sasser. "I'll buy something at the bakery."

"I bet Virginia Woolf bakes things for her daughter," said Roz.

"In the first place, Virginia Woolf has been dead for more than fifty years," said Mrs. Sasser. "And in the second place, she didn't have any children."

"Well, I bet she would have baked cupcakes for her daughter if she had one," said Roz. "Please, won't you?"

"Maybe Grandma will bake some for you," suggested Roz's mother.

"I'll bake them," said her father. "And Roz will help me. We'll make the best cupcakes the fourth grade ever had. Anybody who teaches high school English should be able to read a recipe and follow directions," he said confidently.

So the evening before Roz's birthday Mr.

Sasser, armed with a cookbook and various ingredients, set to work. Roz was at his side. It wasn't long before Mr. Sasser realized that he needed more than Roz's help. He also needed to borrow muffin tins and vanilla extract and baking powder from his mother-in-law.

"Cooking is more complicated than I realized," he admitted.

Roz loved helping her father. She had recently begun cooking a bit with her grandmother, so she was able to explain a few things, like "cream the butter and sugar together." It meant that you mix them up, but Roz's father thought he would have to go out and buy some cream to add to the ingredients. If he had done that, he would have ruined the cupcakes.

When Roz's mother returned from her evening class, there were two dozen cupcakes sitting on the counter. They were covered with vanilla frosting, which Mr. Sasser had found in a can when he went shopping for the flour, sugar, and eggs that they had used.

"Is this enough for everyone?" asked Mrs. Sasser as she admired the results.

"There are twenty kids in my class, and one for Mrs. Corey," said Roz. "I think I'll give the extras to Mrs. Miller, the librarian, and Mr. Lyons, the gym teacher."

"That still leaves one," said Mrs. Sasser. "Can I sample it?"

"Oh, dear," said Roz. "I was going to bring it to the principal."

Mrs. Sasser took back her request. "He can have it," she reassured Roz. "It will be better for my waistline if he eats it instead of me."

"How will I carry them to school?" asked Roz.

It was a problem. She wouldn't be able to manage them with her backpack on the bus—even though Ozzie would be there to help out.

"I'll drive them over to your school around one o'clock," offered Roz's mother as she helped Roz fit the cupcakes neatly into a large box.

The sun was shining when Roz woke up

the next morning. She opened her birthday gifts with great excitement. She received two books from her parents. One was called *Tales from Shakespeare,* by Charles and Mary Lamb. The other was a story that Virginia Woolf had written years and years ago for her niece. The book was illustrated with beautiful color pictures. Just in case Roz wasn't happy with these book choices, she also received a gift certificate so that she could pick out some paperbacks for herself at the local bookstore. There was also a pair of wonderful new roller skates and a long-sleeve cotton knit sweater. The sweater was blue with white stars on it. Roz put it on and wore it to school. It was going to be a perfect day.

At school, there was an arithmetic quiz, but it was easy. Roz also knew every one of the words, so she got one-hundred percent on the weekly spelling test. She could hardly wait for the rest of the time to pass till after lunch, when her mother would come to the school with the cupcakes.

At 1:10, Mrs. Rogers, the school secretary, buzzed Roz's room. Even before Mrs. Corey answered the intercom, Roz knew what it was. Her mother had arrived at the building.

Mrs. Corey turned to Roz. "Your mother is waiting downstairs in the office," she said.

Everyone in the class looked pleased by this news. In a few minutes all work would be put aside and they would be eating cupcakes and singing "Happy Birthday."

Roz closed her reading book and shoved it inside her desk. Then she hurried out of the room. She smiled as she entered the school office. Roz saw her mother, but she didn't see the big box of cupcakes.

"Oh, Roz," said Mrs. Sasser. "I did the most ridiculous thing. I locked my car keys inside the car and the cupcakes are locked inside, too. The worst thing is that the motor is still running."

Roz couldn't believe it. She wasn't sure that the motor running was the worst thing. What about her cupcakes? "How can we get them out?" she asked.

"Don't worry," said Mrs. Rogers. "I locked myself out of my car just last month.

Mr. Donovan was able to open the car door for me. He'll do the same for you."

Mr. Donovan, the custodian, had already been buzzed on the intercom and told the problem. Now he entered the office. He was holding a screwdriver and a wire hanger. Roz decided that she would definitely give Mr. Donovan one of the extra cupcakes, even if it meant that she couldn't give one to Mrs. Miller, the librarian.

Roz followed her mother and Mr. Donovan outside to the school parking lot.

Mrs. Sasser put her arm around her daughter. "Isn't this silly?" she said, trying to laugh. "It's a *Comedy of Errors.*" Then she explained to Roz that that was the name of one of the stories in her birthday book *Tales from Shakespeare.*

Roz thought it was worse than silly. She watched Mr. Donovan anxiously as he poked at the lock and the front window. Looking through the glass, Roz could see the car keys still in the ignition. On the backseat she could see the large box that held the cupcakes.

Roz went around and tried opening all

the car doors. They were all locked.

Mr. Donovan whistled under his breath as he fiddled with the screwdriver and the hanger.

"I guess I have good news and bad news," he said.

"What is it?" asked Mrs. Sasser nervously.

Roz didn't want to hear bad news. She only wanted good news.

"The good news is that it's very hard to break into your car," said Mr. Donovan. "The bad news is that I can't help you."

Roz pressed her nose against the back window and looked at the box of cupcakes she and her father had made the night before. How could they get them out?

"Let's break the window," she suggested to her mother.

"Oh, no," said Mrs. Sasser. "That's too drastic a solution. I know what we'll do. I'll phone your father at the high school. He'll just have to drive over here with the extra set of keys. He'll find someone to cover his class for him."

Roz smiled with relief. That was a good

plan. The high school wasn't very far away. He could come to her school in just a few minutes and then hurry back to his.

Roz and her mother rushed back into the school building and into the office. "May I please use your phone?" Mrs. Sasser asked the secretary.

"Oh, dear. No luck?" Mrs. Rogers said. She handed the telephone to Mrs. Sasser. "Just push eight to get an outside line," she said helpfully. Roz decided that when they finally got them out of the car, she would give one of the cupcakes to the secretary, instead of to Mr. Lyons, the gym teacher.

Mrs. Sasser called the high school and found herself speaking to Evelyn Weiss, the assistant principal. She asked if Mrs. Weiss would please locate her husband and give him an important message.

"This is an emergency," Roz's mother began explaining. "No. No one is sick. But I locked the keys inside my car, and the motor's running and there are two dozen cupcakes for our daughter's birthday party at school this afternoon locked inside the car. If you see my husband, please tell him to come to the elementary school immediately. Otherwise, Roz can't have her party, and heaven only knows what's going to happen to the motor of the car."

Mrs. Sasser handed the phone to Roz. "Evelyn wants to talk to you," she said. Roz had met Evelyn a couple of times when she went over to the high school with her father.

"Happy birthday, Roz," said Evelyn. "Many happy returns of the day."

"Thanks," said Roz, blinking back the beginnings of tears. "Do you think you'll be able to find my father?"

"I bet he's in the faculty room. I'll send a student to find him at once," said Evelyn. "Now, don't you worry."

Roz hung up the phone. But she did worry. Suppose her father didn't come right away.

Roz and her mother went outside the school building to wait for Mr. Sasser. "It's one-thirty," said Roz's mother, looking at her wristwatch. "There's still plenty of time for the party," she added, trying to reassure her daughter. "I just hope I'm not ruining the car by having the motor idling for so long."

Suddenly, Roz thought of something. "Doesn't Grandma have a set of our keys?" asked Roz.

"Oh, you're right. I totally forgot that. She does," said Mrs. Sasser, and she rushed back into the school building, followed by Roz, to use the telephone again. There was no answer. Roz's grandmother wasn't home.

"Where can she be at this hour?" wondered Mrs. Sasser. "It isn't one of her days to work at the hospital."

"Maybe Ozzie knows where she is," suggested Roz eagerly. She had never before had a reason to be so glad that she and her uncle went to the same school.

Mrs. Sasser turned to the secretary. "Could you buzz my brother to come to the office for a minute? He's Oscar Sims."

"He's in Mrs. Griffin's homeroom," said Roz.

Roz waited anxiously for Ozzie to come

to the office. If he knew where her grandmother was, they could call her there and arrange for her to hurry and bring the keys.

"She told me she was going shopping," said Ozzie when he came to the office and heard their problem. "She's buying a present for Roz. But I don't know what store. Let me see the car," he said. "Maybe I can open the door."

"How can you open it? My mother couldn't do it. I couldn't do it. Mr. Donovan couldn't do it. It's locked," said Roz. The tears were now streaming down her cheeks. When other kids had parties at school they didn't have problems like this. She wondered what was going on in her classroom. She wondered if her teacher was worrying about where she was.

Ozzie, followed by Mrs. Sasser and Roz, went outside. He tried all the doors, just as Roz had done. The car was locked. He tried to slide one of his pennies into the lock, but nothing happened.

"I bet Virginia Woolf never locked her car keys in her car," wept Roz.

"Virginia Woolf didn't know how to drive a car," said Roz's mother. "Oh, honey, don't cry. I know what I can do. I'm going to phone the bakery and have them deliver two dozen cupcakes. That way, at least you can still have your party even if your father doesn't get here in time to open the car for us."

Roz sniffed back her tears. "That's a good idea," she hiccuped. She didn't care if they weren't homemade cupcakes. She just wanted to have her party.

Roz and Ozzie stayed outside while Mrs. Sasser ran into the school to use the office phone for the third time that afternoon.

A red car passed the school building, but it was not Roz's father. A pickup truck, a blue car, a station wagon, and a mail truck passed the school. A police car cruised by.

"Hey! I bet a policeman would know how to open the door," said Ozzie. He began running toward the car and waving his arms. Roz ran after him.

The policeman stopped his car and rolled down the window.

81

"My sister locked the keys inside her car when she drove it over here," said Ozzie. "Can you help us open it?"

"Come off it, kid," said the policeman, looking from Ozzie to Roz. "Your sister is too young to drive a car."

"This isn't my sister. This is my niece," said Ozzie. "My sister is inside the school building. She left the motor running, too," he said to impress upon the policeman the urgency of the situation.

The policeman got out of his car and walked toward Roz's mother's car. He took something out of his pocket and tried to jiggle it inside the car lock. Roz and Ozzie watched. When nothing happened, the policeman walked back to his own car. Roz thought he might have some other tools there. Instead, he called the dispatcher at police headquarters.

"Get someone over to the Sullivan School," he said. "There's a woman locked out of her car, and the motor is still running."

Roz felt more hopeful now. Policemen

82

were allowed to drive faster than regular people. Probably someone would come in just a couple of seconds. She decided she would give the policeman a cupcake instead of giving one to the principal.

Mrs. Sasser came out of the school building. She was surprised to see the policeman. "The woman at the bakery said a delivery truck was just about to come here anyhow, so we won't have long to wait. We'll have the cupcakes in five minutes. Ten at the very most."

"What time is it now?" asked Roz.

"It's five to two," said her mother.

School was over at three o'clock. Roz hoped the cupcakes would arrive before school was dismissed for the day.

A white truck pulled up in front of the school. Big blue letters on the side said *Holiday Bakery*. A man got out and opened the back of the truck. He took out two large white boxes. As he started toward the door of the school building, a red car pulled up right behind the bakery truck. At the same time, a siren could be heard. A police car

with a flashing blue light pulled up right behind the red car.

"It's Dad!" shrieked Roz as she recognized the red car.

The door of the red car and the door of the police car opened at almost exactly the same moment. The man with the boxes from the bakery turned to watch what was happening. Roz and Ozzie and Mrs. Sasser stood watching, too.

Mr. Sasser turned to the second policeman. "I didn't think I was going that fast," he said. "But it's my daughter's birthday and we made cupcakes last night and they're inside the car but the car is locked and the keys are in the car and the motor is running. So I came as fast as I could with the extra keys. But I'm sure I wasn't speeding," he added very quickly.

"I came to open the car," said the second policeman.

"I came with some cupcakes. I think it's for the birthday, too," said the man from the bakery. He shrugged his shoulders and carried his boxes into the school office. Mrs.

Sasser ran after him. She had to pay for the cupcakes she had ordered over the phone, even though she didn't really need them now. Roz followed after her mother.

Inside the office, Mrs. Sasser discovered that the Bakery had sent four dozen cupcakes.

"I'll only pay for two dozen," she argued. "That's all I ordered. I didn't say four. I said two." She turned to Mrs. Rogers, the secretary, to be her witness.

"That's right," said Mrs. Rogers. "I heard her place the order."

"You only have to pay for two dozen, lady," said the man from the bakery. "The other two dozen were ordered by someone else." He looked at the receipt in his hand. "Someone named Evelyn Weiss called in this other order. We're sending her the bill. These other cupcakes are for someone named Roz."

Mr. Sasser came into the school building, followed by the policeman and by Ozzie. Mr. Sasser was holding the box of cupcakes.

It was 2:05.

"Do you realize we now have seventy-two cupcakes?" giggled Mrs. Sasser when she saw all the cupcakes on the desk in the office. "And there are only twenty children in Roz's class."

It was 2:15 when the children in Roz's class were finally given their cupcakes and a chance to sing "Happy Birthday" to their classmate.

"I thought you went home," said Brie.

Roz would have a very long story to tell Brie later. But she couldn't stay in her classroom for long now, because she had to hurry and distribute the extra cupcakes. Ozzie and everyone else in his class got a cupcake. There were also enough cupcakes for each of the policemen and even for each of the men working down at the station house that day. There was not just one extra cupcake for the secretary, but also one for the nurse, the custodian, the principal, the cafeteria aides, and the reading teacher, as well as one for Mr. Lyons, the gym teacher, and Mrs. Miller, the school librarian.

Thanks to Evelyn's generosity, there

were still a few cupcakes left to take home, too.

"I bet Virginia Woolf never had so many cupcakes," Roz said to her mother that evening. Roz and her parents and Ozzie and his parents were all having dinner together to celebrate the occasion of Roz's ninth birthday.

"I bet you are right," said Mrs. Sasser.

"*All's Well that Ends Well*," said Mr. Sasser. That was the name of another one of Shakespeare's plays, and the story was in Roz's birthday book. Before she went to bed that night, Roz read it. She thought her story was better.

7

Ozzie Joins the Girl Scouts

Every Wednesday, instead of coming home from school, Roz remained behind for her Junior Girl Scout meeting. The girls met in the school cafeteria, and Mrs. Conrad and Mrs. Forman were their leaders. They always had planned activities. Sometimes the girls did an arts-and-crafts project. Sometimes they played games, and sometimes they had an outing to some nearby location. One time they went to a senior-citizen center and brought drawings and collages that they had made to the residents. Brie was a Scout member, too, and she and Roz wore their green sashes over

89

their clothes every Wednesday and felt very special all day long.

On the first Thursday of November, Roz went next door before school to tell her grandmother all about the annual Girl Scout cookie sale that her troop was having. She was so excited that she had finished her breakfast much earlier than usual.

"We got our order sheets yesterday, so now we can begin selling the cookies," Roz announced.

She looked at Ozzie, who was sitting at his kitchen table counting raisins into his bowl of oatmeal. "What are you doing?" she asked him.

"You made me miss my count," Ozzie complained. He started again, silently counting raisins. "Fourteen," he said with satisfaction, and he began to sprinkle them over his cereal. "Oatmeal tastes perfect with fourteen raisins. I always have exactly the same number."

Roz was stunned. She had never seen Ozzie eating his breakfast before. And no one she had ever known counted raisins and insisted on always having the same number every day the way she did. And now here was Ozzie doing it, too. What an amazing coincidence, even if he did eat the wrong number of raisins.

Ozzie began eating his oatmeal. "I wish I could sell cookies with you," said Ozzie. "It isn't fair that only girls sell Girl Scout cookies."

"The sheets hold up to ninety names," said Roz, ignoring the interruption. "Mrs. Conrad said she didn't expect anyone to sell to that many people."

"I'll buy a couple of boxes," offered Roz's grandmother.

"There are different kinds," Roz explained. "They have names like Tagalongs and Do-si-dos and things like that."

"Those names are silly. They don't even sound like cookies," said Ozzie.

"I'm going to sell cookies after school today," said Roz.

"Can I go with you?" asked Ozzie.

"Of course not," said Roz. "You're not a Girl Scout. And besides, you just insulted the cookies. You said they sounded silly."

"But I bet they taste good," he said. "I bet I could help you sell loads of them."

"No. I don't need your help," said Roz. "It's going to be lots of fun ringing door-bells around here. I want to see if I can sell more cookies than any of the other girls in my troop."

Ozzie's usually cheerful face looked sad. "It's not fair," he said, scraping up the last of his oatmeal.

"I have a new riddle for you, Ozzie," said Roz's grandfather as he walked into the kitchen. Roz decided her grandfather must keep a supply of riddles just to distract Ozzie whenever necessary.

"Why are baby chickens so dizzy when they hatch out of their eggs?"

Ozzie wrinkled his nose as he tried to guess the answer.

"They have shell shock," said his father.

Ozzie grinned. "Hey, that's a neat one," he said. He went to get his jacket and back-pack for school.

That afternoon Roz succeeded in selling

Girl Scout cookies to Mrs. Menzer and some other neighbors. Altogether Roz had sold a total of fifteen boxes already. She was feeling very good about it.

That night, Roz made plans to go over to Brie's house after school on Friday. They were not going to sell any cookies that afternoon, however. They decided that it wouldn't be fair for Roz to sell cookies in Brie's neighborhood. And it wouldn't be fair for Brie to make sales that afternoon with Roz just looking on.

"So we're going to take the afternoon off and just play together," Roz explained to her mother in the morning before she left for school.

"I could sell some cookies for you while you're away," offered Ozzie. He was waiting to walk to the bus stop with Roz.

"Thanks, but no thanks," said Roz. Ozzie couldn't seem to get it through his head that he wasn't a Girl Scout.

Roz was really looking forward to visiting with Brie. She even asked her mother if she could stay for supper if she was invited.

"Just call and let me know," said Mrs. Sasser. "Daddy or I will come and pick you up when your visit is over."

Roz went home on Brie's bus that afternoon. Arlene, the driver, took Roz's permission slip to ride the bus, and the girls took seats side by side. Roz wondered if Smiling Jack would notice that she wasn't on his bus.

"I'm feeling kind of funny," said Brie.

"What do you mean 'funny'?" asked Roz.

"I think I'm getting sick. My throat is feeling bad. It hurts when I swallow. It started after lunch, and it's getting worse."

Roz didn't know what to do. She wanted to play at Brie's house, but it wasn't a good plan if Brie was sick. She followed Brie off the bus.

"Do you think I should go home?" she asked.

"I guess so," said Brie, nodding her head.

So five minutes after Roz got to Brie's house, she was already waiting to be picked up by her mother.

"You'll have to come another day when

Brie is feeling better," said Brie's mother apologetically. Mrs. Morgan had taken one look at her daughter's flushed face and known at once that she was ill. So Brie went to bed and Roz waited at the front door to go home. She didn't even get a peek at Brie's baby brother, Graham. She hoped next time she could help Brie take care of him.

"It's too bad about Brie," said Mrs. Sasser as they drove home.

"Yeah," said Roz. She blinked her eyes to keep from crying with disappointment. She knew Brie couldn't help it if she was coming down with something. But why did it have to happen today, of all days?

"Let's stop for ice-cream cones," suggested Mrs. Sasser.

"I don't want any," said Roz.

"Gee, you must be getting sick, too," said her mother. But they drove past the ice-cream store and went straight home.

"Well, Ozzie will be glad to see you. He came into the house to give me something and he asked when you'd be home again."

Roz didn't say anything.

"Why don't you try to sell some more Girl Scout cookies this afternoon?" suggested Mrs. Sasser.

Roz had temporarily forgotten about the cookies. Now she brightened. "Mrs. Mc-Cormack wasn't in yesterday. Maybe she's home now." Then Roz had another thought. Maybe she'd let Ozzie go with her after all. He really wanted to, and she knew if she asked him to come along it would make him very happy. She thought about Ozzie and smiled to herself. He could be a pain, but sometimes he was fun, too. And he was always there for her, loyal and friendly, no matter what she said or did.

Roz dropped her backpack in her bedroom and then ran next door to get Ozzie.

"He's not here, honey," said her grandmother. "He can't be far. Maybe he's walking Mrs. Menzer's dog."

"Okay," said Roz. She'd look for him when she went out selling her cookies.

She went back into her house to get the sheet she used to mark her sales. In her bedroom, she looked on the desk. She was sure she had left it there yesterday. But she couldn't find it.

"Mom," she called. "Did you see my order sheet for Girl Scout cookies?"

"No, I didn't," said Mrs. Sasser. She came into Roz's bedroom and looked around. "This room is pretty messy," she observed. "It's no wonder you can't find anything."

"I know I left the sheet here," said Roz. "Look. Here's the envelope with the money I already collected. The sheet should be right next to it."

"Did you take it into the kitchen?" asked Mrs. Sasser. "Or maybe you stuck it inside one of your schoolbooks."

Roz opened her backpack and flipped through the pages in her arithmetic and social studies books. There was no sign of the order sheet.

"It's got to be here somewhere," said Mrs. Sasser.

Roz looked on her bookshelf and on her chest of drawers.

"Why don't you go roller-skating or bike

97

riding or something?" suggested Mrs. Sasser. "Sometimes when I get stuck with my writing, I do something else. Then all of a sudden, a good idea pops into my head. If you go outdoors and get some fresh air, you might suddenly remember where you put the sheet."

Roz didn't really feel like bike riding or roller-skating, especially without Ozzie to keep her company. She went outside and sat on the front step of the house. She waved to Mrs. Menzer, who was walking Samantha. So Ozzie wasn't walking the dog after all. Roz wondered where he could be.

She didn't have to wonder for long. Suddenly, she saw Ozzie coming toward the house. He walked slowly, and he didn't greet Roz with his usual grin. Roz stood up and approached him.

"Here," Ozzie said, pulling something from behind his back. He handed her the order sheet for the Girl Scout cookies.

"Where did you find this?" asked Roz. And then she answered her own question. "You took it from my bedroom, didn't you?"

Ozzie nodded his head. "Yes," he said.

"That's stealing," she accused her uncle. "You have no right to go into my room and take things."

"I didn't *steal* it," said Ozzie. "I just borrowed it. I wanted to help by selling some cookies for you. The only thing is, I found out it's not so easy to sell cookies. I went a couple of blocks from here, where the people don't know us. No one believed that I was really selling Girl Scout cookies. And no one would buy any. There was even one woman who said she would call the police if I didn't stop pretending to be a Girl Scout."

"No wonder," said Roz angrily. "Whoever heard of a boy Girl Scout?" She was all set to start scolding Ozzie, but he looked so miserable that she shut her mouth.

"Listen, Ozzie," she said after a minute of collecting her thoughts. "I know you like me and I know you wanted to help. But just because we're related and just because we live next door to each other doesn't mean that we are always going to be doing the same things together. Sometimes we will and sometimes we won't." She swallowed and caught her breath. "I need privacy. That means you can't just walk into my bedroom and take my things. And it means that if I have a friend visiting, you can't hang around telling chicken riddles."

"Brie likes my chicken riddles," he said.

"She might like your riddles. But that doesn't mean she wants you bothering us when we are doing our homework," said Roz.

Ozzie looked down at his feet. "Don't you like me?" he asked.

"Of course I like you," said Roz. She realized as she said it that she really did like her uncle. She wasn't just saying it to make him feel better. "But," she added, "I like to do some things on my own. And you should do some things on your own, too. I bet there's a Cub Scout group you could join. Maybe you could start a riddle club or a coin-collecting club."

"There is a Cub Scout troop," said Ozzie.

"My mom said she was going to sign me up for it."

"See," said Roz. "That's great. You'll make some new friends your own age and you'll learn some new things and you'll have a good time. And then when you come home from your meetings, you can tell me all about it and I can tell you all about my meetings. Sometimes we'll be together and sometimes we won't. Do you understand what I mean?"

Ozzie nodded his head.

Roz thought of something and began to giggle. "I wonder what would have happened if you had dressed up, like a girl, in my clothes. Maybe you would have been able to fool people into thinking you were really a Girl Scout."

Ozzie started laughing. "I'd look really weird in a skirt," he said.

"Here comes Mrs. Menzer and Samantha," said Roz.

"Are you still selling those cookies?" asked Mrs. Menzer when she reached the front of the house.

"Yes," said Roz. Yesterday, Mrs. Menzer had bought a box of the mint cookies.

"Last night I spoke on the telephone with my daughter. I made plans to visit with her and my grandchildren next month," said Mrs. Menzer. "It just occurred to me that I should buy a few more boxes of cookies. I could take them with me. My grandchildren love cookies. They're nice kids, but they fight with each other all the time. I wish they would get along with each other as sweetly as you two do."

Roz blushed as she filled in the order slip. She didn't always get along so nicely with Ozzie. She would have to try harder, she promised herself.

"They'll learn," said Roz. "It takes time."

8

Ozzie in Another Mess

It was one of those days when Roz was having trouble concentrating at school. Arithmetic seemed so boring that even though she had gotten a good night's sleep, Roz found herself yawning over and over. She began counting the yawns and keeping track of them with little marks on the side of her paper. Four little straight lines and then a slash through them for the fifth. She was just tallying the eighth yawn when she was startled to alertness by a loud bell.

"It's a fire drill," Paul Olson called out with delight.

Immediately, everyone began to agree

and tell one another the same thing. "A fire drill. It's a fire drill."

Mrs. Corey got up from her desk. "It's a fire drill," she agreed. "But it is not a signal for conversation. Everyone get your jackets and line up at once."

Roz rushed with her classmates to the hooks at the back of the room. She grabbed her jacket and got on line. Brie squeezed in next to her. The two girls would be partners walking down the stairs and out into the street.

Everyone was smiling. By the time the fire drill was over, it would be time for lunch. Roz noticed that she wasn't yawning any longer.

As Mrs. Corey's fourth-grade class reached the stairwell, there was a traffic jam of students. Roz recognized Ozzie's teacher, Mrs. Griffin. She stood back, waiting to lead her second graders down the stairs after Mrs. Corey's class. Roz turned her head and saw Ozzie in the line. When he noticed her, he waved.

Roz's class started down the stairs. Midway down the steps, Roz heard the sound of something rattling on the stairs. It was a familiar sound, and she tried to identify it.

"I think Ozzie has spilled his pennies again," Brie whispered to Roz.

Of course. No wonder the sound was familiar. It was just like the time Ozzie's pennies spilled all over the bus. Looking down, Roz could see pennies rolling down the stairs.

"Money!" someone at the foot of the steps shouted out.

"Free money!"

Oh, no, Roz thought to herself. Ozzie has done it again.

Kids pushed out of line and tried to scoop up the coins littering the stairway.

From behind her, Roz could hear Ozzie's voice calling out, "Give them to me! They're mine."

Roz bent down and tried to retrieve some of the pennies for Ozzie. She had managed to pick up only one when she heard Mrs. Corey's voice.

"What's going on here?" Mrs. Corey demanded. She tried to get the students to move along. But the lure of all the pennies on the stairs was difficult competition.

Boys and girls were bending down and picking up the pennies. Even Brie pushed ahead of Roz and picked up a penny. "Did you find any nickels or dimes?" Roz heard one boy ask another.

She wanted to call out and tell them that Ozzie only carried pennies to school. But she was afraid. You weren't supposed to speak during a fire drill. It seemed as if she was the only one who remembered that.

Eventually, all the students moved down the stairs, along the hall, and out the door of the school building. They stood in lines and waited until a bell from inside rang to signal that it was all right to return to their classrooms.

As the students walked along the hallway back to their classrooms, they passed the principal's office.

Sitting outside, waiting for a conference with the principal because of the disturbance he had caused, was Ozzie. He looked small and pale and unhappy. It made Roz feel awful to see him like that.

He looked at her helplessly. Usually when Ozzie saw Roz at school he broke into a huge grin. Sometimes he even called out, though he wasn't supposed to. He always looked so delighted to see her. When she enrolled in *his* school this fall after moving in next door to Ozzie, he had been thrilled. Now, he looked miserable.

Roz felt sorry for Ozzie. He could be a nuisance. He could be a pain. Still, he was her uncle, and living next door to him and getting to know him better, she had learned to like him, too. She knew that he hadn't created the disturbance on the stairs on purpose. Now he had not only lost his money, he had gotten into big trouble. Roz decided she had better go and help him get out of it.

Without even asking Mrs. Corey if she could be excused, Roz left the line and went over to her uncle. "Don't feel bad, Ozzie," she said to him. She grabbed his hand and gave it a squeeze. Then she dropped it and went into the office.

To get to the principal, you had to go through the general office. Luckily, Mrs. Rogers, the school secretary, was now a good friend of Roz's. After all, she had been given not one but two cupcakes when Roz celebrated her birthday two weeks ago. And Mrs. Rogers knew that the boy sitting outside the principal's office was Roz's uncle.

"Ozzie's in big trouble," said Roz.

Mrs. Rogers nodded her head.

Just then the principal, Mr. Houston, came from the hallway, where he had been supervising the end of the fire drill.

"Well, young man," Mr. Houston said, looking sternly at Ozzie. "What do you have to say for yourself?"

Ozzie swallowed hard. It didn't look as if he had anything to say at all.

"He didn't do anything on purpose. Anyone could have a hole in his pocket. He couldn't help it if all those pennies fell out," said Roz.

"I can't think of any reason why someone would bring that many coins to school," said Mr. Houston.

"It's because he's crazy about pennies,"

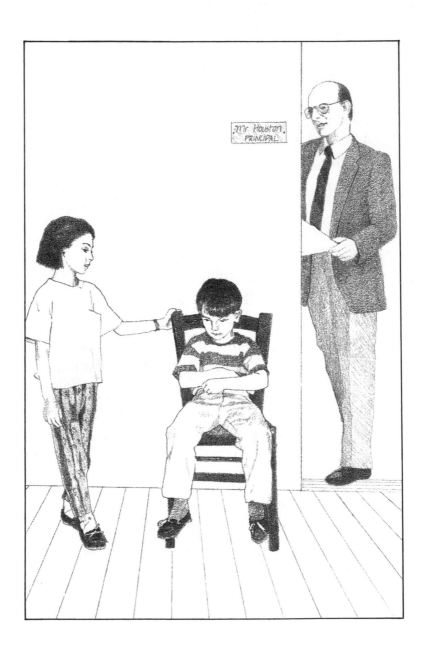

Roz explained quickly. "He collects them. It's his hobby. He has wheat pennies and regular ones. Some of them have letters like *P* or *M* on them. That tells you where they were made."

"*S* and *D*," Ozzie whispered, correcting Roz.

"*S* and *D*," said Roz. "He knows more about pennies than anyone I ever knew."

"I even have a zinc penny," said Ozzie. "Did you ever see one? It's a penny that's made of zinc instead of copper. They made them a long, long time ago, in 1943."

"I remember them," said Mr. Houston. "For some people 1943 isn't that long ago."

"Oh," said Ozzie, beaming. "Do you remember Indian head pennies?"

"I'm not that old," said Mr. Houston sternly. He looked at Ozzie. "Do you realize that fire drills are very serious business around here? A fire drill teaches us how to act in case there ever is a real fire in our school building. Suppose this morning there had been a fire and not a drill. What happened on the stairs could have been disastrous."

111

"I know," said Ozzie, nodding his head.

"What are you going to do to him?" asked Roz. Maybe Ozzie would be kicked out of school.

"I lost all my pennies," said Ozzie. "That's a punishment already," he added hopefully.

"That's true," agreed Mr. Houston. "But you shouldn't have brought them to school. The children who collect stamps or china cats or other things don't bring their collections. You can bring lunch money, but I don't want you to bring so many pennies to school in the future."

"I've been telling him that since the beginning of the school year, but he hasn't listened to me," said Roz.

"Yes, she has," Ozzie agreed.

"What are you doing down here?" asked Mr. Houston, turning to Roz. It was as if he hadn't noticed her before.

"He's my uncle, so I thought I should help him explain things to you. You're not going to punish him, are you?"

"I already lost all my pennies," Ozzie reminded the principal again.

"You're lucky to have a niece who cares for you so much," said Mr. Houston to Ozzie.

Roz blushed at the principal's words.

"All right. Both of you had better return to your classrooms now," said Mr. Houston. "And Ozzie, one more thing," he called as Roz and Ozzie began to walk away.

"Yes?" asked Ozzie. He looked a little nervous. It wasn't too late for Mr. Houston to give him some sort of punishment.

"Be sure and have your mother sew up your pocket," said the principal.

Roz and Ozzie grinned and rushed out of the office. Roz felt her stomach growling. It was time for her class to eat lunch, and she still had to explain to Mrs. Corey why she hadn't returned with the others from the fire drill.

A little later, Roz stood on line to buy her lunch.

Brie stood behind Roz waiting to buy a container of milk. Brie always brought the rest of her lunch from home. "I've got two big cookies in my lunch today," said Brie to Roz. "One of them is for you."

Roz turned and smiled at her classmate. She took the tray with its indentations filled with ravioli with meat sauce and green beans and sliced peaches from a cafeteria aide and reached for a container of chocolate milk. Then she handed a dollar bill and one quarter to the aide at the cash register. The food came to $1.23. As Roz stood waiting for Brie to pay for her milk, she looked at the change she had been given—two pennies. Almost without thinking, Roz turned the pennies over to look at their backs. One of them was a wheat penny—the kind Ozzie was always talking about.

Roz smiled with delight. She'd have to remember to save this penny and give it to Ozzie. Maybe if she watched carefully, she could find a whole lot of them. In fact, maybe she could surprise Ozzie with a roll of fifty wheat pennies for his birthday. That wouldn't be her idea of a special gift, but she knew Ozzie would love it. She had one penny. Now all she needed was to find forty-nine more.

About the Author

JOHANNA HURWITZ is the award-winning author of many popular books for young readers, including *Aldo Applesauce, Rip-Roaring Russell, The Hot and Cold Summer,* and *The Adventures of Ali Baba Bernstein.* She has worked as a children's librarian in school and public libraries in New York City and on Long Island. She frequently visits schools around the country to talk about books with students, teachers, librarians, and parents.

Mrs. Hurwitz and her husband, who live in Great Neck, New York, are the parents of two grown children.